My Daddy is a Guardsman

Written and illustrated
by
Kirk and Sharron Hilbrecht

This book belongs to:

_____

10 9 8 7 6 5 4 3 2 1

ISBN 1-889658-30-8

My daddy is a Guardsman.

Some mornings he gets up really early to do "P.T." That means "physical training." Daddy says he has to exercise to stay in shape for drill, and I help.

We do push-ups...

...and sit-ups.

Sometimes I ride my bike while daddy runs.

He irons his uniform before drill so it will be nice and neat. It is green and has lots of pockets.

He polishes his boots, too. They are shiny and black, and a little too big for me...for now.

Sometimes daddy has to go to the base to train for a long time. He works and trains as an airman.

Daddy says he has to be ready for what-ever job he might have to do. "Guardsmen are busy these days."

"They feed hungry people...

...they fight forest fires...

...they help people who have been in storms....

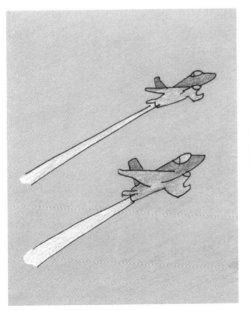

...and they take care of bad guys."

When daddy goes on a mission, he packs up his uniforms, his gear, and his canteen. He wears a big, hard hat, and he carries all of his things in duffel bags.

Daddy says when he goes on a mission, it helps him to learn to be a better Guardsman, but I miss him when he's gone. I wish he had room enough for me.

Once daddy went away for a very long time. Mommy helped me write letters to him, and I drew pictures so he could hang them up and think of us.

We baked cookies to send in daddy's care packages. Chocolate chip are his favorite. Mine too.

While he was gone, daddy wrote to me. I checked the mailbox every day.

When a letter came, mommy read it out loud. Daddy always said he missed us.

When daddy finally came home, he gave us lots of hugs and kisses.

He was really dirty, but mommy didn't make *him* take a bath.

One day, daddy's unit had a picnic for the families.

Daddy says, "It's important to get to know the other families in the Guard.

"These folks can help support each other during missions."

I met some other kids from daddy's unit. I said, "Hi," and told them my name. Soon we were friends.

We talked about what our dads do that make us proud. The others told me what their dads do when they are not at drill.

Tyler said his dad is a pilot, and he flies fast planes.

Christina said her dad is a doctor, and he fixes people.

Michael said his dad is a mechanic, and he fixes big trucks.

Ashley said her dad is a builder who makes giant skyscrapers.

But I said, "I'm proud my daddy is a Guardsman."

"He helps make the world a safe place to live."